SEVEN OF PENTACLES

A MM, TAROT, CITY BOY SMALL TOWN GUY, OPPOSITES ATTRACT, FISH OUT OF WATER ROMANCE

TAROT FANTASIES SERIES
BOOK 7

JAX WILDER

SEVEN OF PENTACLES

Tarot Fantasies Series

RAINBOW QUARTZ PUBLISHING

Published by Rainbow Quartz Publishing

Edmonds WA, 98026

ISBN: 978-1-961714-53-3

First Edition: 2024

Cover design by Miranda Townsend

Interior design by Miranda Townsend

Tarot Card description by Lorelai Hamilton from the book Teenage Tarot – used with permission.

For permissions or inquiries, please contact: Rainbow Quartz Publishing

rainbowquartzpublishing@gmail.com RQPublishing.com

"Just because I talk slow, doesn't mean I'm stupid."
~Jake from Sweet Home Alabama.

Jax Wilder

7 OF PENTACLES

"With patience and persistence, you will reap the rewards of your hard work and dedication," 7 of Pentacles.

KEY WORDS AND PHRASES:

Assessment and Evaluation of progress
Patience and waiting for results
Re-evaluating goals and priorities
Long-term planning and investment
Reflecting on past efforts
Delayed gratification
Harvesting the fruits of labor
Considering alternative strategies
Taking a break to reassess
Feeling a sense of accomplishment, but still having
work to do.

Imagine you've been working really hard on something—a project, a goal, or maybe even yourself. The Seven of Pentacles is like that moment when you pause and take a breather to see how things are going. It's about asking yourself questions like, "Am I on the right track? Are my efforts paying off? Do I need to adjust my approach?"

The Seven of Pentacles isn't just about waiting around. It's about being proactive and making smart choices about where to invest your time and energy. So, when you see The Seven of Pentacles card in a reading, it's like a reminder to take stock of your progress, be patient with yourself, and keep working towards your goals. It's all about trusting the process and knowing that your efforts will pay off in the end.

—Lorelai Hamilton, author of *Teenage Tarot* and *Tarot Tales & Magic Spells*

CHAPTER
ONE

t started with a tremor in my manicured hand—a slight, almost imperceptible shake as I signed off on yet another deal that would pad my already respectable bank account. But by the time I reached my corner office overlooking the New York Stock Exchange, with its grand columns and bustling atmosphere, the tremor had spread—like a crack in a vase that you can't quite believe is real until it shatters in your hands.

I'd built my life around being the best-dressed, best-connected, best-everything in the room. But it turns out, even a wardrobe full of bespoke suits and a Rolodex of power players can't save you from the inevitable—an emotional implosion in the middle of Wall Street. They called it a "nervous breakdown," but I prefer to think of it as my body staging a very dramatic coup.

The solution? Coral Cove. A place that sounds like a retirement community for people who think a wild night involves decaf coffee after 8 PM. My therapist, my boss, and everyone else who thinks they know what's best for me decided that this is where I needed to be. Apparently, when you're on the verge of becoming a cautionary tale, even the people who thrive on your success start to worry.

So here I am, banished to a seaside haven where the biggest thrill is probably a two-for-one sale on seashell necklaces. I've traded skyscrapers for sandy beaches, power lunches for—what? A quaint little café where the biggest decision is whether to order the iced tea or the lemonade?

I'll give it a week before I either lose my mind or simply pass away.

"What am I supposed to do here, Johnny?" I asked, nearly yelling into my cell phone.

"Relax. Get a massage. Go see the sights. Meet some people," he suggested.

"Meet what people? Is anyone here under ninety?" I hadn't seen a single young person in this town since I got here, three whole hours ago.

"Have you even left the hotel yet?" he asked.

I paused and sighed. "No."

Johnny gave me a few more words of encouragement before letting me get on with my evening. I was lucky to have a therapist I could call anytime—considering what I paid, it was the least he could do.

I went to grab my laptop but then remembered I wasn't allowed to be on the internet while I was in Coral Cove. I was only allowed to use my phone for calls. Johnny's rules.

I huffed and tossed the laptop into a pile of clothes across the room before flopping onto the bed.

After a few minutes of staring at the ceiling, I couldn't take it anymore. The idea of spending the evening cooped up in this quaint little hotel room, with its floral wallpaper and the musty scent of decades-old furniture polish, was unbearable. With another heavy sigh, I grabbed my jacket and stepped outside, the cool evening air hitting me like a refreshing slap to the face.

The streets of Coral Cove were almost unsettling in their quietness. No honking taxis, no blaring sirens. Just the gentle hum of conversation from a nearby café and the occasional creak of an old sign swaying in the breeze. I wandered aimlessly, hands shoved in my pockets, trying to make sense of how I ended up in this sleepy seaside town.

As I walked, my eyes caught on a little shop on the corner with a windchime over the entrance. "The Arcane Room," the sign read, with ornate letters painted in a deep shade of purple. The windows were filled with strange objects—crystals, tarot cards, books with titles like *Unlocking the Mysteries of the Universe*. The kind of place that would probably appeal to those who believed in auras and chakras—things I typically scoffed at.

I shook my head, chuckling under my breath. "What is this place, a tourist trap for wannabe witches?"

Still, something about the shop tugged at my curiosity. Maybe it was the bizarre combination of the town's charm and my own boredom, but before I knew it, I was pushing open the door, a small bell jingling above my head.

The interior was exactly what I expected. Dimly lit, the smell of incense hanging heavy in the air, and shelves lining the walls with everything from tarot decks to jars of herbs. A large display case wrapped around the center of the room, covered with bowls filled with stones that supposedly held some sort of mystical power. A few candles flickered on a table near the back, casting shadows that danced across the wooden floor.

"Welcome to the Arcane Room," came a voice from behind the counter.

I turned to see a woman emerging from a curtain that separated the front of the shop from whatever lay beyond. She was seemingly ageless—forties, maybe—with dark hair pulled back into a messy bun. Bright red lipstick contrasted sharply with her pale skin. Her arms were covered in tattoos—intricate designs of moons, stars, and other symbols I didn't recognize, snaking up from her wrists to disappear underneath the sleeves of her loose, flowing blouse.

"Uh, thank you," I said, a nervous smirk tugging at the corners of my mouth.

"That is quite the suit," she said, circling me, taking me in. She chuckled softly, her eyes crinkling at the edges. "You must be a city boy who's found himself lost in our little slice of paradise."

I blinked, taken aback by her bluntness. "How'd you know?"

"Lucky guess," she said with a wink. "Or maybe it's written all over you. Either way, welcome. I am Ms. Vesper."

"Brad," I nodded at her, almost a bow. "So, what is this place? A shop for… mystical supplies?"

Ms. Vesper leaned on the counter, resting her chin in her hand. "These 'mystical supplies,'" she said, her tone teasing but not unkind, "are a collection of tools and treasures for those seeking a little more out of life. Everything here is meant to help people connect with the world around them in ways they might not have considered before."

"Right," I said, trying not to roll my eyes. "And you really believe in all this?"

Her smile softened. "Belief is a funny thing. It's not always about whether something is real or not. Sometimes, it's about the meaning we give to it. But you didn't come in here to listen to me wax philosophically, did you?"

"Honestly, I don't even know why I came in," I admitted, glancing around the shop again.

"Maybe you're looking for something you didn't know you needed," she suggested, her eyes twinkling with mischief. "Maybe you're looking for an exciting kind of experience."

I shrugged. "Maybe."

"Well," she said, pushing off the counter and moving to a table near the curtain she came from. "How about you pull one of these tarot cards for me? Just for fun."

I hesitated, but the boredom I felt earlier was already fading, replaced by a strange sense of anticipation. "Alright," I said, surprising even myself. "Why not?"

Ms. Vesper smiled, her hands deftly shuffling the deck. "That's the spirit," she said. "Let's see what the cards have in store for you, city boy. Go ahead and draw one."

I reached out, a weird tingling sensation in my fingertips as I grabbed the first card I touched and pulled it out. I raised the card to show a man standing with a stick staring at a bunch of circles with stars in the middle.

"Ah, the Seven of Pentacles," Ms. Vesper said. "This symbolizes patience, hard work, and the fruits of your labor. It's a reminder that sometimes you need to take a step back and assess what you've sown, to see if it's truly worth the effort you've invested."

My mouth twisted slightly, one corner tugging upward in a grimace of disbelief. That definitely rang true for me, but I mean, so could any of the cards. Probably. "So, now what? Do I pull another one? What do I do with that information?"

"You get some tea," she said.

"Tea?" I raised an eyebrow at her.

"Follow me," she said, reaching out for my hand. Today was a day of new experiences, and I followed her into a white room, void of any décor aside from a large leather chaise lounge in the middle of the room.

"Sit," Ms. Vesper instructed. I did what I was told and was surprised by the softness. "The Arcane Room offers a certain experience. A magical... getaway, if you will. Have some tea, and you will be transported to your wildest fantasy. Fear not, no matter how long your experience lasts, only twenty minutes will have passed here."

She handed me the tea, and I looked up at her. This was probably how people ended up murdered. I looked back at my cup of tea, a pale yellow color that smelled like a flower bouquet. Oh well, you only live once, as the kids were saying. "Bottoms up," I said, and chugged my tea in one gulp.

CHAPTER
TWO

The tea was warm, but not so hot that it burned on its way down my esophagus. The relaxation was instant. I looked over to where Ms. Vesper had been standing to hand her my cup, but she was gone. I looked down at my hand, and my cup was gone. In fact, everything was gone.

A field stretched out before me, a tangled, sodden landscape where the earth seemed to merge with the water in a murky embrace. The ground was uneven, spongy underfoot, with patches of shallow water that reflected the dull, overcast sky above. Tall reeds and cattails swayed gently in the humid breeze, their tips rustling softly like whispers from the bayou. Moss-draped cypress trees stood sentinel at the edges, their gnarled roots twisting above the surface, creating eerie, shadowed alcoves where the swamp life thrived.

The air smelled like damp earth and decaying vegetation, a heady mix that clung to the back of my throat. Every now and then, a splash echoed in the distance as something unseen disturbed the stillness of the water. The field buzzed with the incessant drone of insects, punctuated by the occasional croak of a bullfrog or the distant call of a bird. It was a place teeming with life yet steeped in an almost unsettling stillness, where time seemed to slow, and the line between water and land blurred into one endless, swampy expanse.

I looked down at my feet and saw my black shiny shoes sinking into a shadowy puddle, the wetness finally sneaking inside, drenching my socks. "Damn it, not my Pradas," I whined, lifting my soggy foot from the water only to realize there wasn't a dry place nearby to put it down.

A loud, strange sound buzzed in the distance, growing louder. I looked around to see the source, a strange boat-like object coming toward me. The boat glided over the swampy field with a strange grace, its flat deck skimming across the water's surface. The loud buzz of the fan engine filled the air, a jarring contrast to the otherwise eerie stillness of the swamp. As it drew closer, I could make out the figure aboard —a man, tall and broad-shouldered, his shirtless torso gleaming with a thin sheen of sweat. His overalls hung low on his hips, worn and dirty, but clinging to him in a way that suggested comfort rather than neglect.

My breath caught in my throat as the boat pulled up alongside me, the man cutting the engine with a practiced hand. He was swarthy, his skin tanned and roughened by the sun, with dark, tousled hair that fell just past his ears. His face was strikingly beautiful, with chiseled features and piercing eyes that seemed to see right through me. But it was the nose ring—a small gold hoop glinting against his rugged appearance—that caught me off guard. It seemed out of place on a man like him, yet somehow, it fit perfectly, adding an unexpected edge to his allure.

He leaned forward, resting a muscled forearm on the edge of the boat as he looked me over, a slow, lazy smile spreading across his lips. "Well, well, looka wah we got here," he drawled, his voice thick with a Cajun accent that rolled off his tongue. "A city boy, lost in the swamp, messin' up his fancy shoos."

I flushed, trying to regain my composure. "Not exactly lost," I replied, though the waver in my voice betrayed me. "Just… exploring."

He chuckled, the sound low and rich, as if he found the whole situation amusing. "E'splorin' huh? Dats wah you call it?" He straightened up and offered me a hand. "Name's Beau. Beau Ducre. But folks 'round here just call me Beau."

I hesitated for a split second before taking his hand. His grip was firm, the callouses on his palm rough against my smooth skin. "Nice to meet you, Beau," I managed, trying to ignore the way my heart was pounding in my chest. "I'm…"

"Brad. I know who you are," he interrupted, his grin widening with a knowing glint in his eye.

My heart skipped a beat. How did he know my name? But before I could ask, Beau was back at the controls, steering the boat through the winding waterways with an ease that suggested he'd been doing it all his life. The swamp closed in around us, the tall grasses and drooping moss casting long shadows as the sun began its descent.

We pulled up to a small shack perched on the edge of the bayou, barely visible among the trees and overgrowth. It was a shabby thing, patched together with weathered wood and corrugated metal, looking like it had seen more than its fair share of storms. A faint smell of smoke and something earthy hung in the air, and I could hear the distant croak of a bull-frog somewhere in the distance.

"This is your place?" I asked, trying to keep the judgment out of my voice. It was a far cry from the penthouse suite I was used to, and I couldn't help but feel a twinge of discomfort at the thought of stepping inside.

Beau turned to me, that easy grin still plastered on his face as he hopped off the boat and onto the rickety wooden dock. "Yessir, dis here's home," he said, giving a casual shrug as if the shack was just another extension of himself. "She ain't much ta look at, but she keeps da rain off my head an' da gators outta my bed. 'Sides, it's all 'bout what's inside, non?"

I could barely understand him.

I hesitated for a moment, but there was no turning back now. I followed him onto the dock, trying to ignore the creak of the old wood beneath my feet.

Beau led the way to the front door, which looked like it was salvaged from a scrapyard and hastily nailed into place. He pushed it open with a creak, revealing a dimly lit interior that smelled faintly of wood smoke and herbs. It was shabby chic inside, with walls lined with shelves crammed full of jars, books, and strange trinkets that I couldn't even begin to identify. A small wood-burning stove sat in the corner, with a cast-iron pot bubbling away on top, filling the room with a savory aroma.

"C'mon in," Beau said, motioning me inside. "Ain't gonna bite ya, non." He chuckled softly as he noticed my hesitation. "Less ya ask me to, dat is."

I stepped across the threshold, trying to adjust to the sudden change in atmosphere. The shack was cramped and cluttered, a far cry from the sleek, minimalist-styled spaces I was accustomed to, but it had a strange, cozy warmth to it. Beau seemed at ease here, moving around the space with the confidence of knowing every inch of it.

He disappeared into another room for a moment and returned with a pair of dry socks and a rag. "Here," he said, handing them to me. They were thick, warm woolen socks. "Get ya feet dry, an' I'll see what I can do 'bout dem fancy shoes a'yours."

I took the socks and rag, grateful for the dry warmth, even if the socks themselves were a far cry from my usual cotton blends. As I peeled off my wet socks and slid on the new ones, I couldn't help but feel a mix of frustration and curiosity. What the hell was I doing here, in this backwater bayou, with a man who seemed more myth than reality?

"So," I started, trying to mask my skepticism, "how'd you know who I am?"

Beau glanced up from where he was kneeling by the stove, carefully placing my Prada shoes near the heat to dry. "Ain't hard ta figure out," his accent as thick as the bayou air. "Dis place? It's where folks end up when dey need lil' somethin' more den wha da city can give 'em. An' you? You got 'dat look, like you ain't quite sure why ya here, but sumptin' brought ya all da same."

I blinked a few times, my ears trying to make sense of the words he threw at me.

Nothing.

"Huh?" I grunted.

"Dis your fantasy," he said, his inflection almost kid-like.

I scoffed, leaning back against the wall, the rough

wood scratching my back. "This is not my fantasy," I said, more to myself than to him. "If anything, this is a nightmare."

Beau just smiled, that easy, knowing grin that suggested he knew more than he was letting on. "Maybe dat's da point," he hissed softly. "Maybe it's 'bout findin' what ya need, even if it ain't wha ya want."

I opened my mouth to argue, to dismiss the words as the ramblings of a man who'd spent too much time alone in the swamp, but something stopped me. Another idea wormed its way into my mind, one that felt more comfortable, more in line with how I saw the world. Maybe I was here to help Beau—show him a few things from the city. After all, who better to introduce him to a different way of life than someone who'd perfected it?

"Maybe," I said slowly, testing the idea as I spoke, "maybe I'm here to help you."

Beau's eyes sparkled with amusement as he stood up, dusting off his hands. "Help me, huh?" he repeated, his tone teasing and half curious. "An' how ya figger dat?"

I straightened up, feeling a flicker of my old confidence returning. "Maybe you need a little refinement," I said, my voice firming up. "A little lesson in living… upscale."

Beau let out a deep, rich laugh that filled the small shack. "Well now, ain't dat a thing,""he said, shaking his head with a grin. "Go on, Brad, give it a shot. Teach me all 'bout bein' a proper city gentleman."

I smirked, giggling a little as I thought about how Beau would be my "pretty woman." This could be fun, but where to even start with this guy? I looked him up and down. "Perhaps we start with a shower."

"I like where dis is goin'," he said, and unbuttoned his overalls, letting them sink to the floor with a thud. Beau stood there in all his glory, exposed to me.

My jaw dropped.

CHAPTER
THREE

"Y ou gonna join me, then?" Beau asked, tilting his head toward the bathroom.

I looked around the shack, feeling the rough edges of the room press in on me, then back at Beau. He stood there with easy confidence, as if the idea of sharing a shower was the most natural thing in the world.

"Ain't nobody here but us," Beau said, winking at me. "You can help me get nice and clean fo' ya."

My heart pounded in my chest, the suggestion hanging heavy in the air between us. The room was already filled with the humid warmth of the shower, and the idea of stripping off my clothes, letting the water wash away the swamp, was becoming more tempting by the second.

Without another word, I began to unbutton my shirt, each movement deliberate as I tried to keep my composure. Beau watched me with an intensity that sent a bolt of electricity through me. His eyes followed my every move as I shrugged out of my shirt and folded it neatly on the chair by the sink. I slipped off my trousers next, laying them gently beside the shirt, and then my underwear, the cool air brushing against my skin as I stood there, exposed and vulnerable in the dim light of the bathroom.

Beau, still wearing nothing, stood there with his muscular frame adorned with sun-kissed rough skin, slick with sweat and dirt. He possessed a rugged, untamed beauty that felt as natural and raw as the wildness of the swamp surrounding us.

I stepped closer, the heat from his body mixing with the steam in the air, and we stepped into the shower. I reached for the bar of soap resting in the basket that hung from the showerhead. Beau turned toward the shower, stepping under the spray of the water with a satisfied sigh as the warm water cascaded over his broad shoulders, washing away the grime and much of the bayou.

I followed him, the water hitting my skin like a hot embrace as I lathered the soap between my hands, creating a rich, fragrant lather that filled the small space with the scent of fresh herbs and cedarwood. Beau turned to face me, his dark eyes gleaming with desire as he took a step closer, his heat melding with mine under the spray.

Slowly, I reached up and began to work the lather

across his chest, my hands gliding over his rough skin, feeling the hardness of his muscles beneath my fingers. Beau closed his eyes, a low hum of pleasure escaping his lips as I moved the soap in slow, deliberate circles, rubbing away the dirt and sweat, leaving only clean, slick skin in its place.

I continued down his torso, my touch firm yet gentle, every movement deliberate, every inch of him becoming more intoxicating as I explored the contours of his body. The water mixed with the soap, creating trails of suds that rolled down his chest, over his abs, and down his legs, pooling at his feet in a swirl of soap and dirt.

I took a step back to look at him. Beau was lean but strong, his muscles looked carved by nature rather than by a gym. His body was adorned with random tattoos, clearly impulsive choices, yet on him, they were endearing.

Beau's hands found my waist, pulling me closer until our bodies were pressed together, his wet skin against mine sending a jolt of pleasure through me. He leaned in, his breath against my ear as he muttered, "Ya got a good touch, cher."

I could feel his hands moving, sliding down my back, the roughness of his palms contrasting with the smoothness of the water-slicked soap. He took the soap from my hands and worked it between his own before slowly running them across my chest, mirroring the motions I had just made on him. The feeling was electric, every touch sending sparks of pleasure through my body as he took his time, savoring every inch of me.

The scent of the soap mingled with the steam, filling my senses with the fresh, earthy aroma of cedar and pine. I could feel the tension draining from my body as Beau's hands moved lower, tracing the lines of my hips, the curves of my thighs, until he was exploring every part of me.

Beau stepped back into the water and pulled me along to warm us back up. After a thorough rinse, we separated again, and he motioned toward the soap. "You gonna help me soap up, or I gotta do dat myself?" he said with a wink.

I could only nod as I reached out with my soapy hands and continued their sensual exploration of his body. The water cascading along his torso, following the contours of his muscles, washed away everything but the heat of the moment. Every touch, every movement, was slow and gentle, building a tension between us that felt like it could snap at any moment.

I lathered up more soap and placed my hands back on his sides. I worked up along his torso, feeling the softer, more sensitive skin. Beau let out a low moan as I moved my way up his sides. He raised his arms above his head, and I moved into his pits.

Beau closed his eyes, enjoying wash. He threw his head back and let out another low moan, almost a growl. His reaction sent a thrill through me, the vulnerability making my pulse quicken. The water poured over us, amplifying the sensation of my hands gliding over his skin, the soap making every movement smooth and deliberate. Beau's muscles flexed under my touch, his body responding to every gentle press of my fingers.

I moved up along his arms, tracing the sinewy lines, feeling the strength beneath the surface. I worked over his shoulders, down the curves of his biceps, before circling back to his chest.

Beau's breath hitched, his body leaning into my touch. His skin was warm under my fingers, and the combination of the steam and the heat radiating between us made the space feel smaller, more enclosed, as if we were the only two people in the world. His chest rose and fell with his deep, steady breaths, each one punctuated by a low, growling moan that sent shivers down my spine.

I continued to explore him, letting my hands slide lower, tracing the defined lines of his abs, feeling the way his muscles tensed and relaxed beneath my touch. He lowered his arms, bringing his hands to rest on my shoulders, his grip firm but gentle as he guided me lower, the water washing over my head.

His hands moved to cup my face, tilting my head back slightly so that I was staring up at him again. There was a raw intensity in his gaze, a mixture of desire and something deeper, something that felt like understanding or even acceptance. Without a word, he leaned over, his lips capturing mine in a slow, sensual kiss, the kind that makes you forget where you are, lost in the feeling of the moment.

The kiss deepened, his tongue sliding against mine in a dance that matched the slow rhythm we'd built between us. We broke the kiss, and he stood back up. My eyes followed his body from his nose ring, down his strong torso, and landing on his girthy cock.

Beau's cock was a vision of perfection. His girth, length, and veiny texture made my mouth water. I looked back up at him.

"It's okay to look an' touch, cher," he said, giving me a coy wink.

I reached out with my freshly soaped hands and grasped him. I wrapped my hand around the middle of his shaft and worked my way to the base, letting the soap slick my hand across him. Then, I stroked back toward his tip, letting the soap coat his entire length. On my second stroke inward, I applied more pressure to my grip.

Beau let out another one of his deep moans. Keeping my pressure steady, I stroked out to the tip of his cock again, gently tugging at his foreskin. Applying a little more pressure, I slicked my fist back down his shaft to the base. I could feel him swell and harden in my palm.

Beau murmured something under his breath, but I didn't catch it. I kept going, his engorged shaft in my hand, stroking him down and back up again, faster and faster. His back arched, and his hips thrust into my fist. Faster and faster, I stroked him, feeling him shift and squirm under my touch.

With a loud, primal groan, he came, his load shooting all over my face. I instinctively closed my eyes, feeling the hot, sticky fluid drip down. Before I could react, I heard Beau say, "Lemme get dat fo' ya."

Beau bent down and licked his mess off my face. I watched him through one open eye as he lapped up his cream, then swallowed it down. I was stunned, my jaw slack, and then I was shocked again by how turned on I was. He reached down, stuck his hands under my arms, and lifted me to my feet as if I weighed nothing. He pulled me back into the running water to rinse my face. I felt his rough yet gentle hands washing me clean.

He pulled my face close to his and kissed me once again. When we finally broke apart, both of us were breathless, our foreheads resting together as the water, still warm, continued to rain down on us. Beau's lips brushed my cheek, his voice a low, gravelly whisper. "Dat's da best clean I ever had, cher," he said softly, his voice laced with satisfaction.

I was too stunned to speak, but I couldn't help the smile that tugged at my lips—a mix of satisfaction and something deeper, something more complicated that I wasn't ready to name yet. Finding my voice, I managed to say, "I'm glad I could help."

We stood there for a moment longer, grounding ourselves in the reality of the moment, even though it felt like something out of a dream. Eventually, Beau reached for the shower controls, turning the water off with a final, satisfying hiss. The room fell quiet, the only sound our breathing, the space still filled with steam and the lingering scent of soap.

"So, what's da next step in becomin' a refined gentleman?" Beau asked, a cocky grin spreading across his face.

CHAPTER
FOUR

Beau stepped out of the shower first, grabbing a towel and tossing it to me before wrapping another around his waist. His easy grin was back, though there was something softer, more open in his eyes now. "Reckon I'm clean enough for ya now, cher?" he said, his accent as thick as ever.

"Why do you keep calling me cher?" I asked, hoping to convey the playful charm in my heart.

"It's short for *mon cheri*. It's Creole for *my dear*. It's a term of endearment," he explained. "Oh, *shabbow*! Look at me, using endearment—like a fancy five-dollar word."

Beau leaned in and gave me a quick kiss on the mouth. "I think it's working after all...," he said and danced out of the bathroom.

I nodded, still processing everything that had just

happened, the mix of emotions swirling inside me. As I dried off and followed him, I couldn't shake the feeling that something had shifted between us. Something I hadn't expected but couldn't ignore.

As I stepped out of the bathroom, towel wrapped around my waist, I glanced down at my bare feet, already missing the polished leather of my Prada shoes. "I wish I had my clothes," I muttered, half to myself.

Beau, now in the middle of the room, looked up with a twinkle in his eye. "Don't worry 'bout dat, cher. Look over by da door. Reckon ya might find somethin' familiar."

Curious, I walked over to the door and, to my surprise, found a suitcase—my suitcase—propped up against the wall. Relief washed over me as I saw my clothes packed neatly inside, along with a few of my favorite accessories. I pulled out a crisp shirt and a pair of tailored trousers, feeling more like myself already.

But as I held my clothes in my hands, another idea struck me. I glanced over at Beau, who was watching me with that easy grin of his, and a thought began to take shape—half-ridiculous, half-intriguing.

"Hey Beau," I said softly, holding up the shirt. "I think you're ready for step two. How would you feel about trying on some of these?"

He raised an eyebrow, clearly amused by the suggestion. "You want me to put on some o' yer fancy city clothes? Ain't never worn nothin' like dat before."

"Exactly," I replied, my excitement growing. "Come on, let's see how you look in something a little different."

"Alright," he leapt forward, dropping his towel. "Why not? Can't hurt ta try."

I looked away and handed him the shirt.

"You're awfully shy for a fella who just had my slick all over your face a few minutes ago," Beau teased. "It's okay to look, cher. It's all yours."

I watched as he slipped on the shirt, the crisp white fabric a stark contrast against his dark skin. He fumbled with the buttons for a moment with his calloused fingers. Next came the underwear. I handed him a sexy, black brief-style pair, and he slipped them on with ease.

I handed him the next article of clothing—the trousers. He slid into them easily, though they were clearly a new experience for him.

"Dis feels strange," he admitted, looking down at himself. "Ain't never worn no pants dat fit so… snug."

I chuckled, stepping closer to adjust the collar of his shirt, my fingers brushing against the warm skin of his neck. "You'll get used to it. Besides, you look great."

And he did.

I gave him a look up and down, gently tousling

his messy hair until it lay nicely. He looked really sexy in my clothes, but at the same time, something about the outfit seemed off. I couldn't put my finger on it.

Beau glanced at himself in the small, cracked mirror by the door, his expression shifting from mild discomfort to something closer to awe. "Well, I'll be," he murmured, his voice almost reverent. "Ain't never seen myself lookin' like dis before, non."

He turned to face me, his eyes meeting mine, full of vulnerability and pride. "Ya really think I look good in dis, Brad?"

I nodded, unable to keep the smile off my face. "You look incredible, Beau. Like you were made for this."

He grinned and rolled his shoulders back as if trying to settle into the new clothes. "Ain't sure 'bout dat, but I gotta admit, it's nice. Feels… different."

We spent the next few minutes with Beau trying on more of my clothes, each outfit drawing out laughter from both of us. He slipped into a tailored jacket, admiring the way it hugged his broad shoulders, then tried on a pair of my designer jeans, surprised by how comfortable they were despite their fitted cut.

There was something endearing about the way he studied himself in the mirror, as if seeing a different side of himself for the first time.

He adjusted a silk tie around his neck, fumbling

with the unfamiliar knot. I stepped in to help, our hands brushing as I guided him through the process. "It's all in the wrist. Over, under, and through," I explained, showing him how to loop the tie just right.

Beau watched me with a soft smile, his eyes twinkling with something that felt like gratitude. "Ain't never thought I'd be wearin' somethin' like dis, but I gotta say, I like it."

We stood there, side by side, both of us dressed in clothes that reflected who I was, yet somehow made Beau look like he'd been wearing them all his life. The laughter, the teasing, the shared glances—all felt like a breath of fresh air.

Beau caught my eye, a playful glint back in his gaze. "Reckon we oughta go show off dis new look, don't ya think, cher?"

I laughed, feeling lighter than I had in a long time. "Absolutely. Let's go turn some heads."

And with that, we headed for the door, a pair of unlikely companions, dressed to the nines and ready for the night.

The path leading back to town was lined with towering cypress trees, their roots twisting in and out of the murky water that lapped at the edges of the trail. The setting sun cast a warm, golden hue over everything, making the world feel soft and dreamlike.

Beau walked beside me, his usual swagger now replaced with a shy excitement as he tugged at the cuffs of his borrowed jacket. He looked over at me with that mischievous grin I was starting to recognize as his trademark. "So, cher, where we headin'? You gonna show me how da other half lives?"

I laughed, shaking my head. "Something like that. I figure we should find a place to eat, give those clothes a proper outing."

He chuckled, his hand brushing mine as we walked. "Long as I'm wit' you, I don' care where we gonna end up. 'Sides, gotta admit, dis whole fancy getup makes me feel like a million bucks."

The rough, wild edges of the bayou gave way to charming streets lined with old brick buildings, their windows glowing with soft lights. It was a picturesque scene, a far cry from the frantic pace of the city, but there was something undeniably appealing about it.

I scanned the street, looking for a place that felt just right. That's when I saw a small upscale restaurant tucked between two quaint shops, its name elegantly displayed in gold lettering above the door. "Le Mistral," it read, promising a mix of French elegance and Southern charm.

"This looks perfect," I said, nodding towards the entrance.

Beau followed my gaze, his eyes widening as he took in the sight. "Well, I'll be," he murmured, clearly awed. "Ain't never been to no place like dis before."

"First time for everything," I said with a smile,

pushing the door open and gesturing for him to step inside.

The interior was just as refined as I had hoped. Le Mistral was dimly lit with soft, amber lighting that reflected off the polished wood floors and white tablecloths. The scent of freshly baked bread and rich sauces filled the air, mingling with the low hum of conversation. Beau hesitated at the entrance, his eyes darting around as if unsure whether he belonged in such a place.

But I gave him a reassuring nudge, leading him to a table near the window. "You're going to love this," I promised, pulling out a chair for him before taking a seat across the table.

As we settled in, a waiter approached with a smile, handing us each a menu. Beau stared at his, brow furrowed as he tried to decipher the elegant script and unfamiliar dish names. "Don't know none of dis," he admitted with a sheepish grin.

"Let's make a deal," I suggested, leaning in conspiratorially. "I'll order for you, and you can order for me. That way, we both get to try something new."

Beau's eyes lit up, his smile returning full force. "Now dat's a plan I can get behind." He glanced at the menu again, then back at me, clearly excited for the challenge. "Alright, cher. Let's see what fancy foods you think I'll like."

I scanned the menu, my eyes landing on a dish

that I knew would be perfect for him—something rich, flavorful, and undeniably sophisticated. "How about the pan-seared duck breast with a port wine reduction, served alongside truffle-infused pommes purée and a medley of haricots verts and heirloom carrots?"

Beau's eyes widened. "I only understood da words duck and carrots, but alright."

He studied the menu with a seriousness that was both endearing and amusing, his lips moving slightly as he sounded out the names of the dishes. After a moment, his face lit up with a grin. "Alright, Brad. How 'bout we go wit' somethin' a lil' closer to home. How you feel 'bout some gumbo and boudin balls?"

I couldn't help but laugh; I didn't understand what he was getting for me either. "Sounds perfect."

When the waiter returned, we placed our orders, exchanging amused glances as we handed over the menus. As we waited for our food, Beau's eyes kept wandering around the restaurant, taking in every detail as if he were afraid he might miss something. There was a sense of wonder in his gaze that made me see him through new eyes.

"So, dis what y'all do in da city?" he asked, leaning back in his chair. "Dress up all fancy-like, go to places like dis, eat food wit' names ya can hardly pronounce?"

"Pretty much," I replied with a chuckle. "It's

about the experience, I guess. But honestly, it's more fun being here… with you."

Beau flashed me that lopsided grin again, his hand resting on the table just inches from mine. "I'm glad I'm here wit' you."

Our food arrived, and we both laughed as we dug into our unfamiliar dishes, each of us trying to make sense of the new flavors and textures. Beau's eyes nearly rolled back in his head as he tasted his duck. "*Shabbow!*" he exclaimed. "Dis… dis is somethin' else."

Meanwhile, I found myself pleasantly surprised by the gumbo and boudin balls—the flavors bold and comforting, a far cry from the usual fare I was accustomed to. We shared bites of each other's meals, laughing as we compared notes and joked about how perfect the evening was turning out to be.

By the time we finished, both of us were full and happy, the atmosphere between us relaxed and warm. We paid the bill and stepped back into the cool night air, Beau slipping his hand into mine as we walked back.

"Dat was somethin' else, cher," he said, low and content. "Never thought I'd enjoy a place like dat, but I gotta admit, it might have been the company."

"I'm glad you liked it," I replied, giving his hand a gentle squeeze. "You too are something else. Thank you for sharing that with me."

Beau leaned in and planted a quick kiss on my

cheek. "Yer a sweet talker, Brad. But I ain't complainin'."

The walk back to Beau's place was filled with easy conversation and laughter. As we stepped inside his place, the familiar scent of wood smoke and herbs greeted us, grounding us back to each other.

Beau slipped off his jacket, hanging it on a hook by the door, and turned to me with a smile that made my heart skip a beat. "Reckon it's time ta get comfy again, don't ya think?"

I nodded, following his lead as we both began to shed the fancy clothes.

CHAPTER
FIVE

Beau pulled me close, his arms wrapping around me in a warm, reassuring embrace. We locked eyes, and I couldn't resist any longer—I pulled him to me, pressing a passionate kiss onto his lips.

Beau responded with an intensity that took my breath away. His lips were firm yet soft against mine, moving in perfect sync as the heat between us began to build. The warmth of his skin seeped into mine, his hand roaming up and down my back, pulling me closer until there wasn't an inch of space left between us.

As our tongues met, sliding together in a slow, deliberate dance, a surge of desire made my head spin. My hands found their way to the buttons of my shirt he was wearing. I unbuttoned one and slipped a finger beneath the fabric, exploring the hard planes of his chest. His skin was warm and despite its roughness, his muscles tensed under my touch. I ran my hands over the ridges of his abs, savoring the feeling of his body responding to me.

I unbuttoned the rest of his shirt, and Beau let out a low, throaty moan as I pulled it from his arms, breaking the kiss just long enough to tug it off and toss it aside. His eyes darkened with desire as he pulled me back to him, his lips crashing against mine with renewed fervor. His hands were everywhere— tangling in my hair, gripping my shoulders, sliding down to my waist as he pressed me against him.

My own shirt was gone in an instant, lost some- where in the flurry of movement as Beau's hands continued their exploration. He traced the lines of my chest, his fingers brushing over my nipples, sending jolts of pleasure through me. I gasped against his mouth, the sound swallowed by a kiss as his tongue explored every inch of my mouth with a hunger that matched my own.

We stumbled back toward the bed, our lips never breaking apart as we moved together, shedding the last remnants of clothing in a haze of heated passion. My pants fell to the floor, quickly followed by Beau's, and then we were skin to skin, his warm body pressed against mine, his erection brushing against my thigh as we finally collapsed onto the bed.

Beau hovered over me, his hands braced on either side of my head as he looked down at me, his eyes blazing with an intensity that made my heart race. He leaned down, his lips trailing hot, open-mouthed kisses along my jaw, down to my neck, sucking and nipping at the sensitive skin until I was arching up against him, desperate for more.

My hands roamed over his back, tracing the contours of his muscles, feeling them ripple beneath my touch as he continued to explore my body with his mouth. He kissed his way down my chest, his tongue flicking out to tease my nipples, making me gasp and writhe beneath him. Every touch, every kiss, sent waves of pleasure coursing through me, the tension between us building to a fever pitch.

I ran my fingers through his hair, gripping it tightly as he moved lower, his lips brushing over my abdomen. I jumped slightly at the cold touch of his golden nose ring. The anticipation was almost unbearable, making my entire body ache for him.

Beau seemed to sense it, his hands sliding down to my hips as he looked up at me, a wicked grin spreading across his face. "Ya taste so good, cher. Can't get enough of ya."

I tugged him back up, capturing his lips in another searing kiss, the need between us growing with every passing second. His hands explored every inch of my body, his touch tender yet demanding, driving me to the edge without pushing me over.

We rolled together on the bed, our bodies tangled in a heated embrace, kissing, touching, exploring—

every moment building higher and higher. The walls echoed our heavy breathing, the scent of our arousal filling the air as we continued to stoke the fire between us.

Beau's lips found mine again, his kiss softer this time, more languid as he pressed his body against mine, our erections brushing together, sending a shudder of pleasure through me. His hands cupped my face, his thumb brushing over my cheek as he pulled back just enough to look into my eyes.

"Yer somethin' else, Brad," he said, his voice thick with emotion. "Ain't never felt like dis before."

I smiled up at him, my heart swelling with emotions. "Me either," I admitted quietly.

We stayed like that for a moment, just holding each other, our breathing slowing as the intensity of the moment settled into something deeper. Beau's hands stroked my sides, his touch soothing, grounding me in the reality of what was happening between us.

Beau resumed his exploration, his kisses trailing lower and lower. He hovered, drawing gentle circles with his tongue around my navel. His chest hovered above my cock, brushing it gently with the tufts of his chest hair. He moved down to my cock and kissed the tip.

In one quick movement, he took all of me into his mouth. Beau's sudden movement sent a shockwave through me, my breath catching as the warmth of his mouth enveloped me completely. The contrast between his earlier tender touches and the sudden, overwhelming sensation left me gasping, my hands instinctively gripping the sheets beneath me.

He paused for a moment, letting me feel the fullness of the moment. His tongue pressed against my dick, swirling in slow, deliberate motions that made my head spin. The sensation was almost too much, but before I could catch my breath, he began to move again, his mouth sliding up and down my length with a tempo that was both torturously slow and incredibly intense.

His hands gripped my hips, holding me steady as he worked, his mouth creating a delicious friction that made it impossible to think, to do anything but feel. The way he moved was unhurried, as if he was savoring every second, every reaction he pulled from me. And gods above, he was pulling reactions from me.

My hips bucked instinctively, seeking more of the sensation he was delivering, but Beau held me firm, his control over the situation only adding to the heat building inside me. The gentle scrape of his stubbled jaw against my skin, the soft sounds of his mouth on me, and the pressure of his hands on my hips combined into an inundating wave of ecstasy that had me teetering on the edge.

Beau pulled back slightly, his tongue teasing the sensitive underside of my cock before taking me in again, his pace quickening, the suction of his mouth increasing. I could feel the heat in my middle building, coiling tighter and tighter with every movement, every flick of his tongue, every slide of his lips.

My hands moved from the sheets to his hair, fingers tangling in his soft strands. The need inside me grew with every passing second. I was close—so close—and Beau knew it. My fingers tightened in his hair.

But then, just as I was about to tip over the edge, Beau pulled back, releasing me from his mouth. I gasped, the sudden loss leaving me heaving, my entire body trembling for release.

He looked up at me, that devilish grin on his face, his eyes dark with desire. "Not yet, cher," he said, his Cajun drawl driving me wild. "Ain't done suckin' at ya yet."

With that, he began his descent again, his mouth and hands moving in tandem as he kissed his way back up my body, tracing the lines of my hips, my stomach, the curves of my chest. Each touch was electrifying, heightening my senses, accentuated by the feeling of his erection brushing against me as he made his way up.

As Beau's mouth found mine again, he kissed me with a hunger that was evident in the hard length pressing into me. He laid down, pressing his weight against me, our bodies slick with sweat and desire. His hands roamed my body, as if he were committing it to memory, and I responded in kind. The need inside me was almost unbearable now, every nerve ending alive with the anticipation of what was to come.

"Ya feel good, Brad," he murmured. "Real good. You want me ta finish ya off?"

I nodded, too lost in the sensation to form coherent words, and he returned to my middle. His lips curled around my cock, taking me further down his throat than before. As the tip of my cock met the back of his throat, he only took me deeper. The tightness of his throat took my breath away. He held it for a few seconds and then began thrusting, deep, wet, and tight into his mouth.

Quicker and with growing urgency, he moved my cock in and out of his mouth. Each thrust sent a jolt through my body. The pressure was building with every second, every expert flick of his tongue, and every deep, wet pull of his lips. My body shook, my muscles tensed as the waves of pleasure rolled over me, growing stronger. Beau's eyes met mine, his mouth full of me. He increased the pace, his mouth working with practiced skill.

The tightness in my abdomen grew unbearable. "Beau," I gasped, "I'm close, so close."

He didn't slow down, didn't let up for even a second. If anything, he only intensified his efforts, his mouth moving faster, his throat tightening around me as he pushed me closer to the brink. The pressure inside me built to a crescendo, my entire body trembling as I felt the orgasm rising, unstoppable.

And then, with one final thrust, I was there, exploding into his mouth with a force that left me quaking, my vision going white as the orgasm consumed me. Beau took it all, his throat working around me, swallowing every last drop as I pulsed inside his mouth.

He held me there, his mouth still wrapped around me, milking every bit of my release until I was completely spent. Finally, he pulled back, his lips releasing me with a soft, wet sound, and looked up at me with a satisfied grin, his lips glistening.

I collapsed back against the pillows, my chest heaving as I tried to catch my breath, my mind still reeling from the aftershocks. Beau crawled up beside me, his hand resting on my chest, his touch grounding me as I slowly came back to myself.

"Ya taste even better than I thought," he said, his voice low and rough. He leaned in, pressing a gentle kiss to my lips, and I could taste myself on him, the lingering sweetness of my release mingling with the saltiness of his skin.

I wrapped my arms around him, pulling him close, feeling his body against mine, the connection between us stronger than ever. We lay there together, tangled in each other's arms, the room filled with the sound of our breathing as we basked in the afterglow, content and utterly spent.

For a moment, neither of us spoke, simply enjoying the quiet intimacy that had settled between us. Beau's fingers traced lazy patterns on my chest, his touch soothing and tender. I felt a deep sense of peace, of belonging, like everything in that moment was exactly as it should be.

"Yer somethin' else, Brad," Beau murmured, his voice filled with emotion. "Ain't never felt this way before."

I looked into his eyes, seeing the vulnerability there, and my heart swelled with affection. "Me neither, Beau. Me neither." We stayed like that, holding each other close, letting the world outside fade away.

CHAPTER
SIX

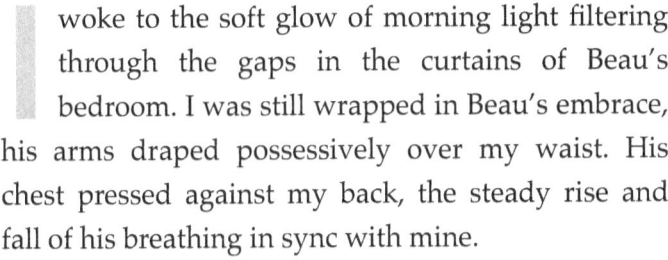

I woke to the soft glow of morning light filtering through the gaps in the curtains of Beau's bedroom. I was still wrapped in Beau's embrace, his arms draped possessively over my waist. His chest pressed against my back, the steady rise and fall of his breathing in sync with mine.

For a moment, I didn't move, savoring the quiet intimacy of the moment. The feel of his body, the comforting weight of his arms, the way his breath tickled the back of my neck—it all felt so right. It was a far cry from the sterile mornings in my penthouse, where the only sounds were the distant hum of the city and the occasional buzz of my phone. Here, in this little place on the edge of the bayou, the world felt slower, softer, and infinitely more real.

I realized this was the first time I had reflected on my life in New York since arriving here. The relentless pace, the constant push to succeed, to be better, faster, more successful—it was as if I had been trapped in a race with no finish line. I had pushed myself so hard because I thought that was what it meant to be alive, to be valuable. But the truth was, I was running myself into the ground, consumed by the need to prove something—to the world, but mostly to myself. The stress had become a constant companion, an unyielding pressure that drove me forward but also crushed me under its weight. Here, in the quiet of the bayou, I could finally see how much it had taken from me—the joy, the peace, the ability to simply be without the nagging voice in the back of my mind telling me I wasn't enough.

I shifted slightly, turning in his arms so I could see his face. Beau was still asleep, his features relaxed, a small smile playing on his lips as if he were dreaming of something pleasant. I hoped he was. The morning light made his skin glow, highlighting the angles of his face, the stubble on his jaw, and the tousled waves of his hair. He looked peaceful, content, and in that moment, I couldn't help but feel a rush of affection for this man.

I reached up, touching him gently on his forehead, my fingers lingering on his skin, marveling at how he felt beneath my touch. Beau stirred slightly, his eyes fluttering open, and when they met mine, my heart skipped a beat.

"Mornin', cher," he murmured, his voice husky

with sleep. He pulled me closer, nuzzling his face into the crook of my neck. "Ya sleep good?"

"Better than I have in a long time," I admitted, my fingers tracing lazy circles on his back. "You?"

He chuckled softly, the sound vibrating against my chest. "Ain't never woke up feelin' dis good before. Must be 'cause I got ya here wit' me."

We lay there for a while, wrapped in each other's arms, content to let the world outside pass us by. Eventually, Beau shifted, propping himself up on one elbow as he looked down at me with his signature grin. "Ya know, I been thinkin'," he began, trailing his fingers down my side. "How 'bout I take ya out into the bayou today? Show ya a lil' more 'bout my world."

I raised an eyebrow, curious but also slightly wary. "Okay…"

Beau chuckled, giving me a wink as he climbed out of bed and began pulling on his clothes. "Don't worry, cher. I'll protect ya. Now, git dressed. We got us an adventure ta start."

I pulled on my clothes with a mix of anticipation and nerves. By the time we were both dressed, the sun filtered through the windows as if blessing the day ahead.

We stepped outside, the humid air wrapping around us in an embrace. Beau led the way, his hand slipping into mine as we made our way through the dense foliage, the ground soft and spongy beneath our feet. The bayou was alive with sound and color, the morning light glinting off the water, making it sparkle like a thousand diamonds.

As we climbed aboard his boat, I couldn't help but feel a mix of excitement and nervousness. The boat was small and rustic, much like everything else about Beau's life here, but it felt sturdy underfoot. Beau handed me a life jacket, which I accepted with a smile, though he didn't put one on himself. "You're not wearing one?" I asked, raising an eyebrow.

"Nah, I been on dis water all my life, cher. I trust it, an' it trusts me," he replied with a wink, his voice brimming with confidence. "But don't you worry. I'll keep ya safe."

With that, we pushed off from the shore, the boat's engine sputtering to life as Beau expertly guided us through the winding waterways of the bayou. The morning mist hung low over the water, adding a mystical quality to the scenery. The thick canopy of trees overhead filtered the sunlight, casting dappled shadows on the surface of the water, which shimmered like liquid gold.

As we glided deeper into the bayou, Beau began pointing out various plants and animals with the enthusiasm of someone sharing a deeply cherished secret. "See dat over dere?" he said, nodding toward a cluster of low-hanging branches draped with moss. "Dat's Spanish moss. It don't harm the trees, just hangs out like a lazy ol' ghost. My grandmère used ta say it was the hair of spirits who couldn't move on."

I leaned in closer, intrigued by the way the moss swayed gently in the breeze. "It's beautiful," I murmured, captivated by the ethereal quality of the landscape. "Your grandmother sounds like she had some interesting stories."

"Oh, she did, cher," Beau replied with a grin. "She was full of 'em. She used ta tell me stories 'bout dis place, how the bayou's alive, breathin' and feelin' just like you an' me. Said if you listen close enough, you can hear its heart beatin'."

I looked out at the water, suddenly aware of the symphony of sounds around us—the distant croak of frogs, the rustling of leaves, the soft lapping of water against the boat. It did feel alive, vibrant with a life force that was palpable. "Do you believe that?" I asked, turning back to Beau.

He paused for a moment, his eyes scanning the horizon. "I do," he said softly, his voice tinged with reverence. "Dis place… it's in my blood. I feel it here," he placed a hand over his heart. "Every time I step out into the bayou, I feel like I'm comin' home."

His words struck a chord in me, and I found myself in awe of his connection to this place. It was a love so deep and intrinsic that it defined him, and in that moment, I realized how much I admired him for it. "You're really passionate about this place, aren't you?" I said, more a statement than a question.

Beau smiled, a soft, almost shy expression that made my heart skip a beat. "Yeah, I reckon I am. Dis place raised me, taught me everythin' I know. It's wild an' untamed, but it's also home. I can't imagine livin' anywhere else."

We continued our journey, and Beau's voice took on a storytelling cadence as he shared more about the bayou. "See dat tree over dere? Dat's a cypress. They say cypress trees are the oldest livin' things in the bayou. Some of 'em been 'round for hundreds of years. Grandmère used ta say they were the guardians of the bayou, watchin' over everythin' that happens here."

I looked at the towering cypress trees with newfound respect, their gnarled roots twisting in and out of the water like ancient, wise sentinels. "It must be amazing, growing up surrounded by all this," I said, feeling a pang of envy for the peace and beauty of his world.

"It is," Beau agreed, his eyes sparkling with pride. "But it ain't always easy. The bayou's beautiful, sure, but it's also dangerous. Gotta respect it, or it'll remind ya who's really in charge."

"Like with the gators?" I asked, remembering the stories I'd heard about alligators lurking in the murky waters.

"Exactly," Beau said with a nod. "Gators, snakes, even the weather—out here, ya gotta be ready for anythin'. But dat's part of the beauty, too. Keeps ya on yer toes, makes ya appreciate what ya got."

After a while, we reached a small clearing where the water was calm and still, the only movement the gentle ripples caused by our boat. Beau cut the engine, and the sudden quiet felt profound, like we had entered a sacred space. He knelt by the water's edge, his movements slow and deliberate as he scanned the surface with a practiced eye.

"Now, ya gotta be real quiet, cher," he whispered, his voice low and serious. "Gators are real quick, but I'm quicker. Jus' follow my lead."

"A gator? Are you serious?" I whispered back, my heart rate spiking at the thought.

"Serious as a heart attack," he replied, grinning widely, a hint of mischief in his eyes. "But don't ya worry none, ain't no danger. I'll be right dere wit' ya. Now be quiet."

I swallowed hard, trying to calm the nerves that fluttered in my stomach. Beau's confidence was reassuring, but the idea of coming face-to-face with an alligator still sent a thrill of fear through me. I watched him move with a quiet grace that belied his usual easy-going nature, his focus entirely on the water.

For a few tense moments, nothing happened. The water was still, the bayou eerily silent as if holding its breath. Then, I saw it—a small gator, barely two feet long, gliding just beneath the surface. Its movements were smooth, almost lazy, but there was something undeniably predatory about the way it cut through the water.

"There he is," Beau whispered, his voice so soft it was almost inaudible. "Now watch closely."

Before I could even blink, Beau's hand shot out like lightning, his fingers closing around the gator's snout with a speed and precision that left me breathless. He lifted the creature out of the water, holding it carefully as it thrashed in his grip, its tail whipping back and forth.

"Gotcha," he shouted, a triumphant smile spreading across his face as he turned to show me his prize. "Ain't he a beauty?"

I stared at the gator in awe, a mix of fear and fascination bubbling up inside me. "You caught it... just like that."

Beau laughed, clearly enjoying my reaction. "Jus' like dat, cher. Now, lemme show ya somethin'." He held the gator up to me, his hands steady as he guided me to touch the rough, scaly skin. "Feel dat? Dey're tougher than dey look, but dey still need respect. Ain't no harm in 'em, long as ya know how ta handle 'em."

Tentatively, I ran my fingers over the gator's skin, the texture rough and prehistoric under my touch. There was something strangely beautiful about it, a reminder of the raw, untamed power of nature. And as I stood there, with Beau guiding my hand, I couldn't help but feel a deep sense of connection—to the gator, to the bayou, and to the man beside me.

"Ya done good, cher," Beau said softly, his eyes meeting mine with a warmth that made my heart swell. "Reckon yer a natural."

I smiled, feeling a rush of pride and affection. "Maybe I am," I replied, my voice soft and cracking slightly.

Beau released the gator back into the water, watching as it quickly disappeared beneath the surface. Then he turned to me, his hands finding their way to my waist as he pulled me close, his lips brushing against my neck.

I giggled, wrapping my arms around his neck and pressing my forehead against his. "This is absolutely incredible."

"What is?"

"This moment. This experience. You," I admitted, leaning in to kiss him.

We stood there for a moment, wrapped in each other's arms, the world around us fading away as we lost ourselves in each other's touch. Eventually, Beau pulled back, his eyes filled with love. "C'mon, cher. Let's keep movin'."

"Do we have to?" I asked.

"What ya got in mind?" he said, raising an eyebrow at me.

I leaned forward, grabbing his face with both of my hands, and kissed him deeply. I tugged at the hem of his shirt, pulling it up over his head. My fingers ran up his chest as I held him in our kiss.

He managed to pull my shirt off, our kiss only breaking long enough for the fabric to slide past my face. Our tongues battled wildly in our mouths, urgent and needy. I could feel my erection swelling inside my jeans. I pressed myself up against him, feeling his hardness against me.

My kiss moved from his lips to his cheek, then around to his neck just below his ear. I suckled at the soft skin there before moving up to his ear. "Can I fuck you?" I whispered gently.

"I thought ya'd never ask," Beau replied, quickly stripping off his jeans and pulling his underwear down with them. My hands trembled slightly as I unbuttoned my jeans, the cool air brushing against my skin as I pushed them down, joining Beau in a state of nakedness. The sun bathed us both, mingling with the heat radiating from our bodies as I stepped closer to him, my heart pounding.

Beau reclined against the flat surface of the boat, his legs spreading slightly to make room for me as I settled between them. His hands found my hips, guiding me closer until our bodies were flush, the sensation of his skin against mine sending shivers of pleasure through me.

I looked into his gentle eyes once more and realized why I was brought here. And maybe, just maybe, I'd be brave enough to tell him.

CHAPTER
SEVEN

Beau caught me staring at him. "What ya thinkin' 'bout?" he asked, his voice a low, teasing rumble.

"Your sexy body," I replied with a grin, leaning down to capture his lips in a hungry, deep kiss as I positioned myself at his entrance. Beau's breath hitched, his grip on my hips tightening as I began to press into him. The tightness and heat of his body drew a low groan from my throat.

The boat rocked gently with our movements, the world around us narrowing to just the two of us—the feel of his body yielding to mine, the way he gasped and moaned as I pushed deeper inside him. Beau's legs wrapped around my waist, pulling me closer as I began to move, each thrust deliberate, designed to draw out every ounce of pleasure from the moment.

"Gods, you feel so good," I whispered against his

lips, my voice thick with desire. I increased the pace, the friction nearly explosive.

Beau's head fell back, his eyes fluttering shut as he let out a low, throaty moan that echoed down the bayou. "Fuck, Brad. Don't stop."

I had no intention of stopping. The feel of him, the way his body moved with mine, the sounds he made—it was all too much. I thrust deeper, harder, the boat swaying beneath us in time with our movements. The gentle breeze of the bayou did nothing to cool the heat burning between us, making the sweat drip down from my chest.

Beau's hands roamed up my arms, his fingers digging into my skin as he urged me on, his breath coming in short, ragged gasps. I could feel the tension building inside both of us, coiling tight, ready to snap.

I shifted my angle, hitting that spot inside him that made him cry out, his voice raw and desperate. "Right there," he gasped, his words almost a plea. "Fuck, Brad… right there."

I focused on that spot, driving into him with a steady, relentless rhythm that had us both on the edge. The boat rocked harder now, the sounds of the bayou drowned out by our grunts, our panting breaths, and the slap of skin on skin.

I could feel myself getting close, the pressure building to a peak. Beau came with a shout, his body shaking beneath me as he pulsed around my cock, the intensity of his orgasm triggering the start of my own. His cum shot out of him, splattering across his chest, and without thinking, I leaned down, licked up a sample of his seed with my tongue.

The taste of him pushed me over the edge. A wave of pleasure crashed over me, leaving me breathless, trembling, and lost in the sensation of being buried inside him as I released. I thrust into him one last time, deep and hard, my body shuddering as I spilled into him.

We stayed like that for a moment, our bodies still joined, our breaths mingling in the warm, humid air as the aftershocks of our releases slowly ebbed away. The boat rocked gently, the world around us gradually coming back into focus.

Beau's hands slid up my back, pulling me down to rest against his chest, my cock slowly softening as it slipped from his body. My chest felt the slickness of his cum between us, my breath still coming in soft pants. "Shabbow," he said, his voice rough and full of satisfaction. "Dat was somethin' else, cher."

I smiled, pressing a kiss to his neck, a deep sense of contentment settling over me. "Yes, it was."

We lay there on the boat, the sun warming our skin, the sounds of the bayou wrapping around us like a blanket. The intimacy of the moment, the connection we'd just shared, felt like something out of a dream.

Beau's fingers traced lazy patterns on my back as

he held me close, his lips brushing against my temple in a gesture as sweet as it was reassuring. "Reckon we should head back soon," he whispered. "I kinda feel like jus' stickin' here wit' ya, but I gotta be honest. Dem skeeters gonna be comin' out full force here quick."

I laughed, closing my eyes and letting the peace of the moment wash over me. "We better get moving then."

Reluctantly, we picked up our clothing and got dressed as quickly as we could. Beau fired up the boat, and we headed back towards his shack, the engine humming as it cut through the still waters of the bayou.

As Beau guided the boat through the winding waterways, the sun began its slow descent, casting a golden glow over everything. The hum of the fan propeller filled the air, blending with the distant sounds of the swamp—a sound I was beginning to appreciate in a way I never thought possible. I watched Beau at the helm, his easy confidence, the way he seemed so at home here, and I felt a swell of emotion rising in my chest.

We reached his shack just as the last light of day was fading, the shadows stretching long and deep across the water. Beau tied the boat to the dock with practiced ease and helped me onto the wooden planks. The smell of wood smoke and damp earth greeted us as we walked inside, a sense of comfort and belonging settling over me.

Beau glanced over at me, a small smile playing on his lips as he pulled me into his arms, holding me close. "Dat was somethin', huh?"

I nodded, resting my head on his shoulder, feeling the steady beat of his heart against my chest. "Yes, it was. But there's something I need to say, Beau. Something that took me a while to realize."

He pulled back slightly, his brow furrowing in concern as he looked at me. "What's dat, cher?"

I took a deep breath, gathering my thoughts, my hands resting on his chest as I searched for the right words. "When I first got here, I thought this fantasy was all about me trying to change you—making you more like me. Bring some of the city to the bayou. But the truth is, Beau... it wasn't about changing you at all."

His expression softened. "What d'ya mean?"

"I mean, it's me who needed to change," I confessed. "I've spent so much of my life in this frantic, endless race, trying to prove myself, trying to be something... someone I thought I needed to be. But being here, with you, I've realized that what I really need is to slow down, to take it easy. I need to learn to appreciate the little things—the joy in just being, in loving freely. And yes, even touching alligators."

Beau chuckled, tightening his hands around my waist. His gaze didn't waver as he listened, the sincerity in his eyes giving me the courage to continue.

"I was so caught up in my own world, in my own expectations, that I forgot how to really live. But you've shown me that there's more to life than just chasing the next goal, the next achievement. You've taught me to find joy in the simple things, to appreciate the beauty in the world around me, and to love without holding back. And for that, Beau, I can't thank you enough."

He was silent for a moment, his eyes searching mine as he processed my words. Then, slowly, a warm, genuine grin spread across his face. He leaned down and pressed a soft, lingering kiss to my lips.

"Ya don' gotta thank me, Brad," he murmured against my mouth. "I'm jus' glad I could share all dis wit' ya. Ain't never thought I'd meet someone like ya, but now dat I have, I can't imagine it any otha way."

I smiled, my heart full as I wrapped my arms around his neck, pulling him closer. "Me neither, Beau. Me neither."

We stood there in the quiet of the shack, holding each other, our connection filling the space between us. The world outside was still and peaceful, the sounds of the bayou a gentle reminder of the place that had become my sanctuary.

Finally, Beau pulled back, his hands cupping my face as he looked at me with a serene tenderness. "I'll tell ya what, cher," he said, his voice gentle. "We got plenty mo' time ta take it easy, ta find joy in all da lil' things. But for now, how 'bout we make some supper, light a fire, and just enjoy dis night together."

I nodded, a sense of contentment washing over me. "That sounds perfect."

As we prepared dinner, lighting the fire, and settling into the simple pleasures of the evening, I soaked in the comfort of being with Beau. Later, as we sat on the couch, the flicker of the fire casting warm shadows across the room, I leaned into him, my head resting on his shoulder, and felt a deep sense of peace.

I knew this was just the beginning—of a new chapter, a new way of living for me, one filled with love, laughter, and the kind of tranquility I had been searching for all along.

The flames of the fire hypnotized me, lulling me into a peaceful sleep as the world faded into the comforting embrace of the night.

CHAPTER
EIGHT

blinked myself awake, disoriented, and found myself in a plain white room. The vivid memories of where I had just been lingered in my mind, and for a moment, I felt lost, caught between two worlds. As the confusion began to ebb away, reality slowly settled back in. I remembered coming to the Arcane Room, meeting Ms. Vesper, and drinking the tea that had set everything in motion.

"Take your time getting up," Ms. Vesper's voice floated softly from the door, bringing me back to the present.

I sat up slowly, the simplicity of the room starkly contrasting with the vibrant world I had just left behind. The chaise lounge was comfortable, but it paled in comparison to the warmth of Beau's arms or the gentle sway of the boat in the bayou. I swung my legs over the side of the chaise, planting my feet on the cool floor as I tried to process everything that had just happened.

Beau had felt so real, so alive. The connection we shared was undeniable, transcending the physical and touching something deeper within me. Yet, as I sat there, the reality that I would probably never see him again weighed heavily on me. It was a strange sort of heartbreak, knowing that what we'd shared would remain in that fantasy space, locked away in a memory I would carry with me but never relive.

And yet, with the sadness came a quiet resolve. My time in Coral Cove wasn't over. Beau had taught me so much in those fleeting moments—how to slow down, how to find joy in the simple things, how to live in the present rather than constantly chasing the future. I owed it to myself to take those lessons to heart, to spend the rest of my time here embracing the peace and beauty that this seaside town had to offer.

I stood up, smoothing the wrinkles in my shirt, my thoughts still swirling as I made my way to the curtain. Pushing it aside, I found Ms. Vesper waiting for me, her knowing eyes watching me with the same gentle warmth she had shown before.

"How do you feel?" she asked, her voice a soothing balm to my frayed emotions.

I took a deep breath, letting the air fill my lungs before releasing it slowly. "Different," I admitted, offering a small smile. "Better. But... there's a sadness too."

Ms. Vesper nodded, her expression wise and understanding. "That's natural, hon. Experiences like these can be powerful, even life-changing. They're meant to show you something, to teach you what you need to know. Sometimes, the hardest part is letting go."

I looked down, my thoughts still tangled with the emotions. "I'm not sure I'll ever let go of what I felt in there. But I know now that I needed it."

She stepped closer, placing her hand on my arm with a comforting touch. "That's the right attitude." She winked.

I nodded, feeling both gratitude and sadness swirling in my chest. "Thank you, for everything."

"You're welcome," she said, her smile warm and reassuring. "Is there anything else I can do for you?"

I hesitated for a moment, then reached into my pocket for my wallet. "How much do I owe you for all of this?"

She waved her hand dismissively, her smile widening. "First experience is always free. But if you feel inclined, gratuities are always appreciated."

Without a second thought, I reached into my wallet and pulled out a crisp stack of bills—one thousand dollars. I placed it in her hand, watching as her eyes widened slightly before she looked back up at me with surprise and gratitude.

"This is for everything you've done," I said, my voice steady. "It was worth every penny."

Ms. Vesper's smile softened, a look of deep appreciation in her eyes as she accepted the money. "You're too kind. Thank you."

She tucked the money away and then, with a curious glint in her eye, she asked, "So how did it go? Was it everything you wanted?"

I paused, letting the memories of Beau flood back —his laughter, his love, the lessons he'd imparted, all rushing over me in a wave of warmth and nostalgia. A smile spread across my face as I remembered Beau's playful spirit, the way he made me feel alive and whole in a way I hadn't felt in years.

"Shabbow," I replied, the word rolling off my tongue with deep affection and satisfaction. "Shabbow."

Thanks for reading Seven of Pentacles. If you enjoyed it, please check out Harvesting Love, Steamy MM, Small Town, Second Chance, Thanksgiving Holiday Romance

Falling in love this Thanksgiving season.
Park:
Being best friends with the boss has its perks.
Like a discount on the latest spicy MM romance.
Or the ability to knock off a bit early when a smokin' hot bibliophile pops into the shop.

The day before Thanksgiving, I had a chance encounter with a man that left us both feeling an undeniable chemistry between us.

Instead of the comforting scent of pumpkin pie, this holiday is filled with family anxiety.

Can I convince him to spend a little more time together, even if it's with my crazy family?

Falling in love this Thanksgiving season.

In the charming town of Coral Cove, Park is preparing for another Thanksgiving spent with family—while longing for someone to share his life with. Despite being surrounded by love, Park feels the weight of his loneliness as the holiday season approaches. When a handsome stranger walks into his small bookstore, Park's hope for a holiday romance sparks.

Ben Dawson is trying to escape the pain of losing his fiancé. A year after the tragic accident, he heads to Coral Cove on what was supposed to be their dream vacation. He's not expecting to find anything but bittersweet memories—until he meets Park, the adorable bookstore owner who makes Ben wonder if second chances at love are possible.

As Thanksgiving approaches, Park and Ben's chemistry ignites, leading them both to question their pasts, futures, and the magic of love that just might be waiting for them in the most unexpected of places.

Harvesting Love is a heartwarming and steamy MM romance set against the backdrop of the Thanksgiving season. Perfect for fans of small-town charm, second-chance love, and holiday magic, this book will capture your heart.

Sign up for Jax Wilder's newsletter and receive a collection of unpublished Coral Cove short stories. Meet familiar characters and dive deeper into the love and romance that Coral Cove is known for. Don't miss out on this exclusive content!

Jax Wilder

ALSO BY JAX WILDER

Coral Cove Series

Sleighed by Love

Harvesting Love

Dawning Desire

Knead You Now

Love Rewound

Perfect Lover Spell

Haunted by Her

Tarot Fantasies Series

The Devil's Temptations

Strength of the Beast

Hanged Passions

Six of Cups

Death's Embrace

Queen of Pentacles

Seven of Pentacles

Ace of Wands

Three of Swords

Two of Swords

Lovers In The Veil

Stand Alone Titles

Pride and Prejudice and Witches

ADDITIONAL BOOKS BY RAINBOW QUARTZ PUBLISHING

LORELAI HAMILTON

Find Your Bliss

Teenage Witch's Grimoire

Tarot Reflection Journal

Tarot Refection Journal Coloring The Tarot

The Eclectic Witch's Grimoire

Dream Journal

Teenage Tarot

Tarot Tales and Magic Spells

Arcane In Verse

MIRANDA LEVI

From A Youth A Fountain Did Flow

The Sea Withdrew

A Tear In Time

Mo(ther) Na(ture)

In Orion's Hands

JACKSON ANHALT

From The 911 Files

LORELAI HAMILTON

Find Your Bliss

Teenage Witch's Grimoire

Tarot Reflection Journal

Tarot Refection Journal Coloring The Tarot

The Eclectic Witch's Grimoire

Dream Journal

Teenage Tarot

Tarot Tales and Magic Spells

Arcane In Verse

ISLA WATTS

A Fairy Bad Day

Surprise! You're a Vampire

Gorgeous, Gorgeous, Gorgons

Mork The Handsome Orc

Adopted By Werewolves

Bite Me If You Can

That's The Spirit!

ROSE DAWSON'S BOOK JOURNALS

My Time With The Fairies

Enchanted Escapades

Enchanted Escapades

Dewey Decimal Diaries

Siren's Songbook

Pride and Prejudice

Bibliophile's Bounty

Book of Books Journal

Pages & Passages Reading Journal

Bookworm's Companion Reading Journal & Tracker

ABOUT THE AUTHOR

Jax Wilder is a passionate romance author hailing from a charming small town nestled in the picturesque Pacific Northwest. With a heart full of love and an unyielding belief in the power of happily ever afters, Jax weaves enchanting tales of love and connection that leave readers captivated.

Jax's novels are a reflection of her commitment to celebrating the magic of love, and her characters' journeys mirror the warmth and happiness she has found in her own life. Join her on the enchanting journey of love, passion, and enduring connection through her heartfelt romance novels.